First published in 2015 by Curious Fox, an imprint of Capstone
Global Library Limited, 7 Pilgrim Street, London, EC4V 6LB
Registered company number: 6695582

www.curious-fox.com

CAPG34269

Illustrations by:
Comicup Studio
Carmen Pérez – Pencils
Francisco Figueres Farrès – Inks
Gloria Caballe – Colour

ISBN 978-1-782-02231-2
18 17 16 15 14
10 9 8 7 6 5 4 3 2 1

A CIP catalogue for this book is available from
the British Library.

Printed and bound in China by Leo Paper Group

THERE'S A MOUSE HIDING IN THIS BOOK!

Curious Fox

THERE'S A MOUSE HIDING IN THIS BOOK!

by Benjamin Bird

THAT PESKY PEST IS TOO QUICK!

This time, count to three.
Then turn the page as fast as you can!

ONE ... TWO ...

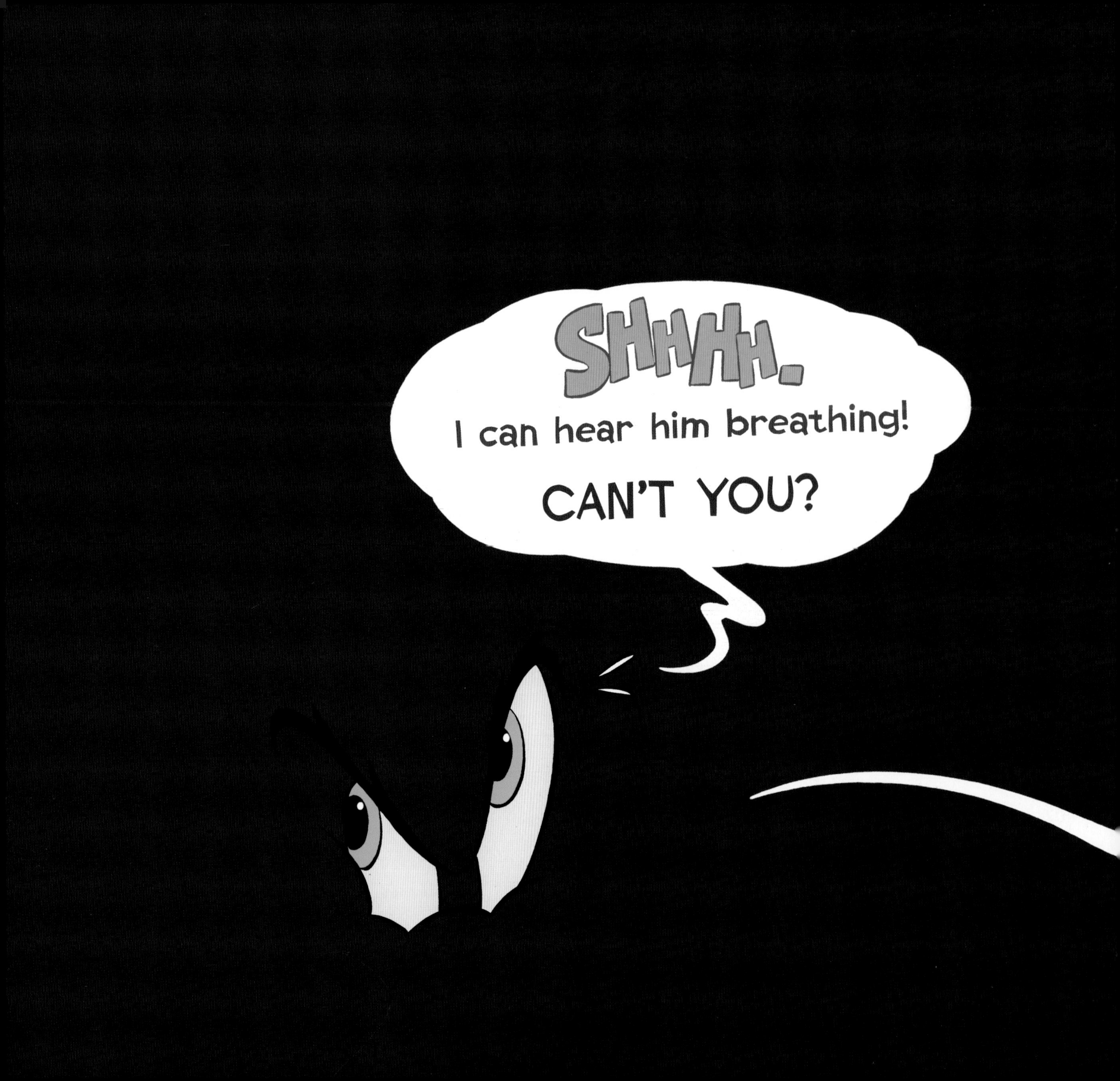
SHHHH.
I can hear him breathing!
CAN'T YOU?

Blow on the page as hard as you can.

BLOW, BLOW, BLOW!

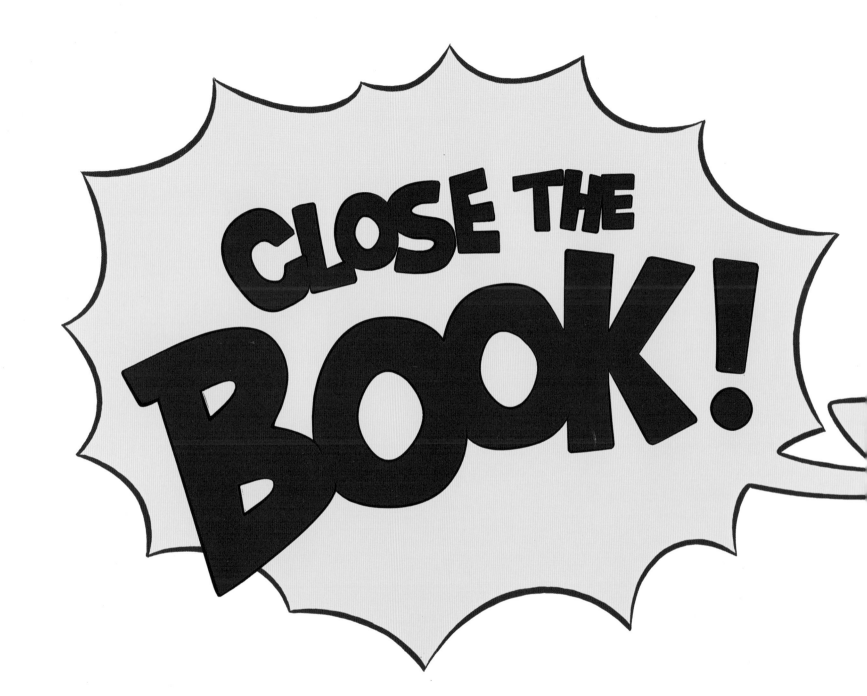

Have you read...

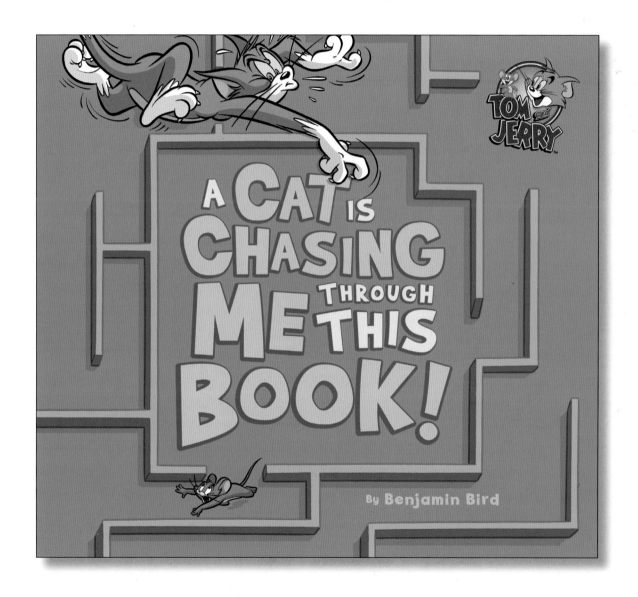

Help Jerry outsmart Tom in this fun, read-aloud picture book featuring your favourite cat and mouse rivals.